INSIDE THE
OLYMPICS

NICK HUNTER

Raintree

CHICAGO, ILLINOIS

www.heinemannraintree.com
Visit our website to find out more information about Heinemann-Raintree books.

To order:

☎ Phone 888-454-2279

🖻 Visit www.heinemannraintree.com to browse our catalog and order online.

Edited by Louise Galpine and Diyan Leake
Designed by Marcus Bell
Original illustrations © Capstone Global
    Library Ltd 2011
Illustrated by Jeff Edwards
Picture research by Elizabeth Alexander
Originated by Capstone Global Library Ltd
Printed in and bound in the United States of America,
    North Mankato, MN

15 14 13 12
10 9 8 7 6 5 4 3 2

Library of Congress Cataloging-in-Publication Data

Hunter, Nick.
  Inside the Olympics / Nick Hunter.
    p. cm.
  Includes bibliographical references and index.
  ISBN 978-1-4329-5488-8 (hc)—ISBN 978-1-4329-5489-5 (pb) 1. Olympics—History. 2. Olympic Games (30th : 2012 : London, England) I. Title.
  GV721.5.H846 2012
  796.48—dc22   2011000916

032012
006621RP

Acknowledgments

We would like to thank the following for permission to reproduce photographs: Alamy pp. **7** (© Ace Stock Limited), **27** (© Robert Harding Picture Library Ltd); Corbis pp. **4** (© Zainal Abd Halim/Reuters), **9** (© Gianni Dagli Orti), **16** (© Bettmann), **23** (© PCN), **24** (© Daniel Deme/epa), **28** (© Kay Nietfeld/epa), **34** (© Sampics), **43** (© Chen Xiaowei/Xinhua Press), **47** (© Peter Macdiarmid/epa); Getty Images pp. **5** (BOCOG), **13** (Harlingue/Roger Viollet), **15** (Hulton Archive), **17** (IOC Olympic Museum/Allsport), **21** (Tony Duffy/Allsport), **20** (Pascal Pavani/AFP), **30** (Stu Forster), **31** (Dan Kitwood), **32** (Nick Laham), **36** (Clive Brunskill/Allsport), **37** (Jerry Cooke/Sports Illustrated), **38** (Daniel Berehulak), **39** (Topical Press Agency), **41** (Streeter Lecka), **50** (Steve Powell/Allsport); 2007 Olympic Delivery Authority (ODA) p. **52**; Press Association Images pp. **18** (AP), **19** (Paul Vathis/AP), **22** (DPA Deutsche Press-Agentur/DPA), **29** (Gareth Copley/Empics Sport), **33** (Tony Marshall/Empics Sport), **42** (Elizabeth Dalziel/AP), **45** (DPA Deutsche Press-Agentur/DPA), **49** (Tony Marshall/Empics Sport), **51** (Ulf Palm/Scanpix), **54** (Greg Baker/AP); Shutterstock p. **11** (© Panos Karapanagiotis).

Upper front cover photograph of the men's 110-meter hurdles semifinals at the 2008 Summer Olympics reproduced with permission of Getty Images (Bill Frakes/Sports Illustrated); lower front cover photograph of the start of the 100-meter sprint at the first modern Olympic Games, Athens, Greece, 1896, reproduced with permission of Getty Images.

Every effort has been made to contact copyright holders of material reproduced in this book. Any omissions will be rectified in subsequent printings if notice is given to the publisher.

Disclaimer

All the Internet addresses (URLs) given in this book were valid at the time of going to press. However, due to the dynamic nature of the Internet, some addresses may have changed, or sites may have changed or ceased to exist since publication. While the author and publisher regret any inconvenience this may cause readers, no responsibility for any such changes can be accepted by either the author or the publisher.

INSIDE THE
OLYMPICS

Contents

Some words are shown in bold, **like this**. These words are explained in the glossary.

Olympic Dreams

This is it. The athletes have been training all their lives for this moment as they step out onto the track in front of 80,000 cheering fans in the stadium. Many millions more are watching on live TV around the world. In the next few minutes, each athlete will find out if they can achieve their goal. For some, the goal was just to be here, in this packed stadium, to compete against the best athletes in the world in the Olympic final. Others will only be happy if they can claim a medal or be crowned Olympic champion.

The Olympic Games are the world's biggest sporting event. The Summer Olympics are held every four years in a different city. More than 10,000 athletes from around 200 different countries come together to compete in the Games. There are more than 300 different events in many sports, from archery to wrestling. Athletes in sports such as skating and skiing also compete every four years in the separate Winter Olympics. The **Paralympic Games** take place just after the Winter and Summer Olympics for athletes with disabilities. For all these athletes, success at the Olympics or Paralympics is their ultimate dream.

▲ These athletes are waiting for the start of the Olympic marathon. After more than 42 kilometers (26 miles) and two hours of running, one of them will be the Olympic champion.

► The Olympic champion does not win huge sums of money. The Olympic gold medal **symbolizes** to everyone that the winners are the best in the world at their chosen sport.

The world's Games

Olympic athletes include everyone from superstars such as NBA basketball stars and multimillionaire soccer and tennis players, to those from the world's poorest countries or war zones, who have overcome huge obstacles just to be there. This mix makes the Olympics a global event like no other. The 2008 Summer Olympics in Beijing, China, were watched on television by 4.7 billion people. That is 70 percent of the world's population.

As London prepares to host the Olympic and Paralympic Games in 2012, this book will look at the story of how the Olympics became such a huge global event. We will discover the sports and the amazing sporting achievements that lie at the heart of the Olympics. The book will also consider some of the controversies that have affected the Olympics. However, before exploring these issues, we will journey back thousands of years to the origins of the Olympic Games.

''You have the dream as a kid of standing on the podium, being a champion … I began rowing at 14 and a year later, someone was saying, 'you're capable of being a champion'—I thought to myself: 'I want to be an Olympic champion.'''

Steve Redgrave, winner of five Olympic gold medals for rowing.

Ancient Olympics

The origins of the Olympic Games can be traced back almost 3,000 years to ancient Greece. The official date of the first Olympics is 776 BCE, although some kind of festival probably happened even earlier. Every four years, people from the many **city-states** that made up ancient Greece would meet at the **sacred** site of Olympia. The Olympic Games were so important that a **truce** was declared in any wars between the states, so that people could travel to the Games without being attacked or captured. Anyone who broke the truce had to pay a fine. King Alexander the Great was fined when his soldiers attacked a man traveling to Olympia from Athens.

"Aren't you scorched there by the fierce heat? Aren't you crushed in the crowd? Isn't it difficult to freshen yourself up? Doesn't the rain soak you to the skin? Aren't you bothered by the noise, the din, and other nuisances? But it seems to me that you ... gladly endure all this, when you think of the gripping spectacle that you will see."

Ancient Greek philosopher Epictetus describes the ancient Olympics

Greek legends said that the Games had been started by the Greek hero Heracles, or that a local king had started them to bring peace to Greece. Whatever the real reason, the Olympic Games were not the only games in Greece, although they were the oldest. Games were also held in Delphi, Corinth, and Nemea. An athlete who was successful at all four festivals was called a *periodonikes*.

The site at Olympia

The first Olympic Games were as much a religious festival as they were a sporting one. Olympia was one of the most sacred places of the god Zeus, the leader of the many ancient Greek gods. The site at Olympia had many temples and religious buildings, including a statue of Zeus that was 43 feet (13 meters) high. The site grew over many centuries to include a stadium for foot races, and other buildings such as a gymnasium, which was the same length as the stadium, for training. The hippodrome was used for races on horseback and chariot racing.

▲ As Greek influence spread across the Mediterranean Sea, athletes traveled to the Olympics from as far away as Spain.

▲ Vase paintings of the ancient Olympics usually show athletes running with no clothes on. The earliest runners probably wore loincloths. The legend is that Orsippos of Megara lost his loincloth while winning the stade race in 720 BCE. After that, everyone started running in the nude.

Ancient Olympic sports

At the first Games in 776 BCE, the **stade** race was the only sporting event. It was a running race of just under 200 meters (655 feet), or one length of the stadium. Other events were added over time, but this remained one of the most important. Athletes who won the stade race were revered almost as sporting gods.

The Olympic program

As the ancient Olympic Games became established, new events were added. At their height in about 100 BCE, the Games lasted for five days. Religious and official ceremonies took place on the first day. The contests began in earnest on day two with the horse and chariot races in the hippodrome. Only the wealthiest people could afford to send a chariot with a team of two or four horses to the Olympics. Crashes happened often, and they could be fatal.

In the afternoon, athletes took part in the ultimate test of their speed, strength, and stamina. In the **pentathlon**, athletes competed in five sports in a day: running, discus throwing, javelin, long jump, and wrestling.

Sacrifice and sprinting

Before the sporting events on day three, one hundred oxen were sacrificed. These oxen were roasted and eaten at a feast later in the day. This custom has not been adopted at the modern Olympics. Running races took place in the afternoon. As well as the *stade* race, runners competed in the *diaulos*, a running race across two lengths of the stadium (or two *stades*), and a long distance race over 20 or 24 lengths of the stadium, called the *dolichos*. Some of the best runners won all three of these races. Today, it would be impossible to imagine the same athlete winning the 100 meters and the 5,000 meters.

Combat sports

On day four, the crowds could enjoy a display of combat sports. Wrestling and boxing were very popular. They were an important part of the training for young warriors. The object of wrestling was for the winner to throw his opponent to the ground three times. The rules of boxing were probably less strict than they are today. Almost any blow with the hand was allowed. *Pankration* was the most violent sport of all. Almost anything was allowed, including arm twisting and strangling. Only eye-gouging and biting were forbidden. The contest continued until one pankratist admitted defeat.

Athletes were naked for most events. However, the final event was the race in armor. Athletes raced the length of the stadium wearing heavy armor and carrying a shield. This was a reminder that, for the ancient Greeks, athletic training was closely linked to keeping the body fit for war. Day five was given over to a procession of the winners, feasts, and celebrations.

LEONIDAS OF RHODES

Leonidas was probably the greatest ancient Olympic athlete. He won the *stade* race, the *diaulos*, and the long-distance race at four Olympic Games in a row between 164 and 152 BCE. This was all the more amazing because all of these events were held on the same day. We know about athletes like Leonidas from coins showing their faces, statues, and the few written records that survive.

*People from **Sparta** were renowned for being fierce wrestlers. One Spartan wrestler said:*

"The other wrestlers are stylists. I win by my strength, as is only fitting for a Spartan youth."

▲ Statues give us information about athletes in the past. This is a Roman copy of an ancient Greek statue of a discus thrower. The original version has been lost.

Rewarding the winners

Big prizes were on offer at many ancient Greek sporting festivals, but not at the Olympics. Winners received a wreath of olive leaves, cut from a sacred olive tree at Olympia. Despite this prize, winning at the Olympics was still the greatest sporting achievement in the ancient world. Winners or their supporters would pay for a statue to be erected on the sacred site at Olympia, and the champions would be given money and honors when they returned to their home states.

Women at the ancient Olympics

One major difference between the ancient Olympics and the modern Games was the fact that all the athletes at the ancient Games were men. Married women were not even allowed to attend the Games. Women did have their own games at Olympia. The Heraian Games, named in honor of the goddess Hera, were also held every four years, but they only included one event—a shortened *stade* race.

One married woman did manage to see the Games. Kallipateira trained her son to victory in the Olympic boxing event. When he won, she was so excited she ran out of the trainers' enclosure, revealing to everyone who she was. Although there were harsh punishments for women attending the Games, Kallipateira was not punished because her father, son, and brother were all Olympic champions. To prevent the same thing from happening again, it was decided that all trainers as well as athletes should be naked when they registered for the Games.

The end of the party

The ancient Olympic Games lasted for more than 1,000 years, but their slow decline began as early as 424 BCE, when thousands of troops had to protect the Olympics from a Spartan army that was threatening to invade. As the Greek civilization became less powerful and united, the Games also suffered. The Romans also loved sports. When Olympia became part of their empire in the 2nd century BCE, the Games were **revived**, although they were briefly moved to Rome itself. The end of the ancient Olympics probably came in 393 CE, when the Roman emperor Theodosius banned all non-Christian festivals.

We would not have the modern Olympic Games if the site at Olympia had not been rediscovered. It was discovered by the Englishman Richard Chandler in 1766, but the first major **excavation** of the site was carried out by the German government, beginning in 1875. A young Frenchman, Baron Pierre de Coubertin, read reports of the discoveries at Olympia. As he learned more about the ancient Olympics, Coubertin became convinced that the time was right to revive the Games.

POLITICS, MONEY, AND BRIBERY

Politics were just as much a part of the ancient Games as they are at the modern Olympics. City-states erected monuments and statues of their athletes, leaders, and military victories to impress their rivals. Chariot races were the main event where wealthy individuals could show off their power. They could enter several chariots to give them a bigger chance of victory. In 372 BCE, when teams owned by one of the judges won both the two-horse and four-horse chariot race, it was decided that judges should no longer be able to enter teams.

▲ The remains of the ancient Olympic site at Olympia can still be seen today. This arch is the entrance to the Olympic Stadium.

Reviving the Olympics

The modern Olympic Games have become such a massive global event that it is easy to assume that this has always been the case. However, the birth and development of the Games was not an easy one. The Olympic Games owe their existence to a French nobleman with a passion for sporting excellence.

Coubertin's dream

Baron Pierre de Coubertin's dream of reviving the Olympics was inspired by reports of the excavations of the ancient Olympic site at Olympia, as well as by a belief in the importance of physical exercise, which was not widely held at the time. Coubertin was able to win others over to his big idea. In 1894, at the Olympic Congress in Paris, delegates voted to hold Olympic Games in Athens, Greece, in 1896.

The project to revive the Olympic Games was supported by King George I of Greece. On April 6, 1896, he opened the first modern Olympics. A new stadium had been built to host the Games on the site of an ancient arena. James Connolly of the United States won the triple jump to become the first Olympic champion. Winners were given a silver medal and a crown of olive branches, an echo of the ancient Olympics.

Local hero

Some events, such as one-armed weightlifting and the 100-meter freestyle swim for members of the Greek navy, did not feature in later Olympics. One event that made its debut in 1896 captured the imagination of spectators more than any other. The marathon had not featured at the ancient Olympics but was inspired by the ancient Greek legend of Pheidippides. He is said to have carried news of the Greek victory at the Battle of Marathon in 490 BCE by running from Marathon to Athens. The first Olympic marathon began in Marathon. After 40 kilometers (almost 25 miles), the runners neared the finish in the Olympic stadium. Local hero Spiridon Louis took the lead and became the most popular winner of the Games.

The Athens Olympics were declared a success, and it was decided to hold the Games in Coubertin's home city of Paris in 1900. However, problems at the next two Games challenged the very existence of the Olympics.

PIERRE DE COUBERTIN (1863–1937)

Baron Pierre de Coubertin was born in Paris, France. As a young man, Coubertin was interested in education. He believed that the mind and body developed together, and was an admirer of the emphasis on competitive sports in the British private school system and U.S. college sports.

In 1894, Coubertin brought together sportspeople and supporters from around the world at a huge banquet in Paris. They voted to revive the Olympic Games. The **International Olympic Committee** (IOC) was set up to organize the first Games. Coubertin became its first secretary-general. The founder of the Olympics was also president of the IOC from 1896 to 1925. Many believe that the Olympics would not have survived without his leadership. When Coubertin died, his heart was buried as part of a monument in Olympia.

Trials and triumphs

The 1900 Olympics were not a success. Coubertin thought that combining them with the Paris World's Fair would make the Olympics into a bigger event. This did not work, as Olympic events were spread over many months. They became just a small part of the World's Fair. Despite these problems, the Paris Games were much bigger than the first Olympics. More than 1,000 athletes took part, including the first female competitors. Charlotte Cooper of Great Britain won the singles tennis competition to become the first women's Olympic champion.

Meet me in St. Louis

After the difficulties in Paris, the next Games needed to make up some lost ground. Unfortunately, the Games in St. Louis, Missouri, repeated many of the mistakes from Paris and added a few of their own. Once again, the Games were held at the same time as the World's Fair and took place over several months. These were the first Games held outside Europe. Only twelve nations sent athletes to the Games, and many events only included Americans. The appeal of the Olympics was not yet strong enough for athletes to travel by sea and land from Europe to the middle of North America. Even Baron de Coubertin chose not to attend.

The Games in St. Louis were the first Olympics at which gold, silver, and bronze medals were awarded. It also welcomed the first African athletes. Two Tswana tribesmen from southern Africa who were attending the World's Fair took part in the marathon. American George Eyser won six medals in gymnastics. This was a remarkable feat, as Eyser's left leg was made of wood.

GREAT MOMENTS

MARATHON MIX-UP, LONDON, UK, JULY 24, 1908

The 1908 London Olympics were not without controversy. Italian Dorando Pietri was leading the marathon as he entered the Olympic Stadium. But Pietri, the crowd's favorite, was completely exhausted and collapsed a number of times on the track. When he fell just short of the finish line, officials carried him across ahead of the chasing American John Hayes. As Pietri was stretchered away, the U.S. team protested, and Hayes was declared the winner because Pietri had been helped. Although he didn't win Olympic gold, Pietri became famous around the world.

After disastrous Games in Paris and St. Louis, the Olympics needed a boost. The next official Games took place in London in 1908, with the first purpose-built Olympic Stadium. These Games and the 1912 Olympics in Stockholm, Sweden, were much better organized and hosted many great performances. However, just as the Olympics were getting established, World War I intervened. The 1916 Games, scheduled for Berlin, Germany, were canceled. Could the Olympics recover from this setback?

BIOGRAPHY

JIM THORPE (1888–1953)

This awesome all-round American Indian athlete won gold medals in the pentathlon and decathlon at the 1912 Olympics in Stockholm, Sweden. It later emerged that Thorpe had received money for playing baseball. At that time, **professional** athletes were not allowed at the Olympics. Thorpe was stripped of his medals. As well as his success at the Olympics, Thorpe also became one of the greats of football in the U.S. Despite being named the greatest American athlete of the first half of the 20th century, he struggled to find work in later years. Thorpe's legend has grown since his death in 1953. The Pennsylvania town where he is buried was renamed in his honor, and his Olympic medals were restored in 1982 after a long campaign.

Between the wars

As the world, and particularly Europe, emerged from the horrors of World War I, the 1920 Olympic Games in Antwerp, Belgium, saw the first appearance of a new Olympic symbol—the flag. The five rings of the flag are now one of the most recognized symbols in the world.

The Olympic Games of the 1920s in Antwerp, Paris (1924), and Amsterdam (1928), were very peaceful compared to what followed. The Olympics gradually became more global, and crowds could witness great athletes in action, such as Finland's Paavo Nurmi, who won nine gold medals on the track between 1920 and 1928. The first Winter Olympics were also held in 1924, when 258 athletes gathered in Chamonix, France, to compete in sports from bobsled to speed skating.

The number of women competitors also increased as track-and-field events for women were introduced in 1928. When some female 800-meter runners collapsed with exhaustion after the race, some people claimed this was evidence that women could not handle longer races. No running races longer than 200 meters were held until the 1960 Olympics.

There were fewer athletes at the Los Angeles Olympics in 1932. This was partly due to the Great Depression (an economic crisis that began in 1929 and lasted for ten years). Also, California was still fairly remote for many athletes in the days before long-distance air travel. These were the first games to use photo-finish technology to decide winners of close races. Unfortunately, it took days to develop the film, so it was not terribly useful.

BIOGRAPHY

MILDRED "BABE" DIDRIKSON (1911–1956)

"Babe" Didrikson was not just a great Olympian; she also became a leading **amateur** golfer and an all-American basketball player. At the 1932 Los Angeles Olympics, Didrikson won gold in the javelin and 80-meter hurdles (pictured), and set a world record in the high jump, although she was **disqualified** on a technicality. She had qualified for all five women's athletics events but could only compete in three.

We are used to the idea of the Olympics as a global event. Athletes fly in from around the world to compete. Transportation in the early days was much more difficult. The New Zealand team took more than nine weeks to travel by sea to the 1920 Olympics in Antwerp, Belgium. Their ship was delayed in Melbourne, Australia, and Durban, South Africa. It arrived just two days before the start of the Games.

Hitler's Olympics

When the 1936 Olympics were awarded to Berlin, Germany, Adolf Hitler's Nazi regime had not yet come to power. Many people knew of Hitler's **racist** views and were unhappy about staging the Games in Berlin. Hitler saw the Olympics as the perfect chance to prove his racist theory that the white Aryan race was superior to others. Jesse Owens had other ideas. The great African-American athlete won four gold medals. Unfortunately, the Olympics were just the start for Hitler. These Games were the last for twelve years, as World War II plunged the world into chaos once more.

▲ Leni Riefenstahl's film of the 1936 Olympics was intended to promote the Nazis' view of the world.

The Global Games

When World War II came to an end in 1945, it left millions dead across the world. There had been no Olympic Games since 1936. Could the Games be revived? The first opportunity to rebuild the Olympics was in war-ravaged London in 1948 (see panel). London welcomed more athletes from more nations than had competed at the Berlin Olympics in 1936. The Games continued to grow, even though world events would get in the way of sports and harmony many times in the postwar period.

Cold War, politics, and terrorism

After World War II, much of the world was divided into two opposing groups of countries, in what became known as the Cold War. The **Soviet Union** and its allies were on one side, and the United States and its allies on the other. Rivalry between these two groups often spilled over into the Olympics, and competition to top the **medal table** was intense.

Other political issues also affected the Olympics. South Africa was banned from 1964 until 1992 because of its government's racist **apartheid** policies. John Carlos and Tommie Smith's Black Power salute drew attention to racial issues in the United States at the Mexico City Games in 1968.

▲ John Carlos and Tommie Smith's Black Power salute at the 1968 Olympics meant that they were sent home by the U.S. national team.

The conflict in the Middle East left its mark on the Munich Olympics in 1972. On September 5, Palestinian **terrorists** stormed the athletes' village, killing two Israeli athletes and taking nine more hostage. All the hostages were killed in a gun battle as the terrorists tried to escape. These events cast a shadow over the Olympics. Security of athletes and spectators became a major issue.

▲ Romanian gymnast Nadia Comăneci won three gold medals in 1976, becoming the first Olympic gymnast to be awarded a perfect score.

The Paralympics

The postwar period also saw the development of the Paralympics for athletes with disabilities. The Paralympics grew out of a sporting event for ex-soldiers with **spinal injuries** that was held at Stoke Mandeville in Buckinghamshire, England, to coincide with the London Olympics in 1948. The event grew, and the first official Paralympics were held in Rome in 1960. The Paralympics are held after the Olympics using the same venues.

BEHIND THE SCENES

"THE AUSTERITY OLYMPICS"

London was an unlikely host city for the 1948 Olympics. Food was still rationed after World War II, and there was no money to stage a huge sporting spectacle. Against the odds, the Games were a success. The great Czech runner Emil Zatopek said the revival of the Olympics was "as if the sun had come out." Athletes were housed in army camps and schools, and brought their own towels. The athletics track at Wembley Stadium was a converted dog-racing track. Despite all this, the Games produced stars such as Micheline Ostermeyer, the French concert pianist who won gold in the discus and shot put events.

The Cold War continued to disrupt the Olympics in the 1980s. The United States called for a **boycott** of the Moscow Olympics in 1980 because of the Soviet Union's invasion of Afghanistan. Many countries followed the U.S. lead, while others, including the United Kingdom and Australia, left it up to individual athletes to decide whether they wanted to attend. In 1984, the Soviet Union and its allies boycotted the Los Angeles games in retaliation. For various reasons, tiny Albania boycotted four Olympics between Montreal, Canada, in 1976 and Seoul, South Korea, in 1988.

With the Cold War over and the end of the apartheid regime in South Africa, Barcelona in 1992 was the first Games since 1960 where all nations could be represented. Since then, the Games have been truly global. Teams come from almost every nation on the planet. Athletes from 79 countries won medals at the 1996 Atlanta Olympics, although the Games were criticized for poor organization and too much influence from commercial **sponsors**. The Games were also affected by a bomb attack that killed one person and injured more than 100.

GREAT MOMENTS

AFRICA UNITED, BARCELONA, SPAIN, AUGUST 7, 1992

Derartu Tulu was the first black African woman to win gold at the Olympics when she won the 10,000 meters in Barcelona. The silver medal went to Elana Meyer of South Africa, a country that was about to elect Nelson Mandela as its first black president after years of rule by the white minority. Their shared joy at the end of the race was seen by many as a symbol of a new beginning for the Olympics, and for Africa.

CARL LEWIS (born 1961)

Carl Lewis came from a family of athletes. His two parents were track coaches. Lewis qualified for the 1980 Olympics but could not compete because of the United States' boycott. He made up for lost time in 1984, winning four gold medals, in the 100 meters, 200 meters, long jump, and sprint relay. This matched the achievement of Jesse Owens in 1936. Lewis didn't finish there. He won two gold medals in 1988 and 1992. In 1996, Lewis won the long jump for the fourth time. He retired in 1997 with a haul of nine Olympic gold medals.

Into the 21st century

For many people, the Sydney Olympics of 2000 were the ultimate mix of a great setting, efficient organization, and sporting greatness. The highlight for many Australian spectators was the victory of **Aboriginal** Australian Cathy Freeman in the 400 meters on the track. In 2004, the Olympics returned to the city of the first modern Games, Athens. The shot put events were even held in the ancient stadium at Olympia.

The Olympic Games in the 21st century welcomes more than 10,000 athletes, as well as thousands of coaches and officials. The cost of hosting such a huge event has grown greatly. In 2008, Beijing, China, put on the most expensive Olympics ever. Estimates put the cost at around $40 billion. Although future Games may not be able to match the costly spectacle of Beijing, there is no doubt that there will be great performers, records will be broken, and controversy will never be far away.

Winter Olympics

The Winter Olympics are also held every four years. Until 1924, figure skating and ice hockey were part of the Summer Olympics. The Winter Games have avoided many of the controversies of the Summer Olympics, although they have had their own issues. The weather was often a big problem at early Games. At the 1928 Games in St. Moritz, Switzerland, a speed skating event had to be canceled because of warm weather. In recent years, artificial snow has been used when there is not enough real snow. However, storms and blizzards can still disrupt the Games.

The first Winter Olympics did not include many of the sports that are now part of the Games. Downhill and slalom skiing were not added until the Garmisch-Partenkirchen Games of 1936. The Winter Olympics have also adapted to developments in winter sports, which have changed dramatically in the lifetime of the Winter Games. Freestyle skiing became an Olympic sport at Albertville, France, in 1992, and snowboarding was a popular addition to the Games in Nagano, Japan, in 1998.

GREAT MOMENTS

TONYA vs NANCY, LILLEHAMMER, NORWAY, 1994

In the months before the 1994 Winter Olympics in Lillehammer, Norway, U.S. figure-skating star Nancy Kerrigan was hit on the knee by an attacker as she left the ice after practice. Her rival Tonya Harding went on to win the national championships and qualify for the Olympics. It soon emerged that Harding was involved in a plot to injure Kerrigan to improve her own chance of getting to the Olympics. Despite this, the rivals appeared together at the Olympics. Kerrigan recovered from her injury to claim a silver medal. Harding could only finish eighth.

▶ Tonya Harding (left) and Nancy Kerrigan were the biggest story at the Winter Olympics in 1994.

▲ Winter Olympic sports can be highly dangerous as athletes reach speeds of around 90 miles (145 kilometers) per hour. At the Vancouver Olympics in 2010, Georgian luge competitor Nodar Kumaritashvili was killed in practice when he came off the track at high speed.

Until 1992, the Winter Olympics happened in the same year as the Summer Games. Since the Albertville Olympics in 1994, the Winter and Summer Olympics have been held in different years. This change was made because of the difficulty of organizing, finding sponsors, and televising two such huge events in the same year.

Snow problem?

The Winter Olympics have always been a smaller event than the Summer Games. This is because, for the most part, only countries that have snow and ice, or mountains, compete in winter sports. This is usually the case, but not always. Jamaica is not a country known for its cold weather. At Calgary in 1988, the Jamaican bobsled team were big stars. They proved that the Winter Olympics could be just as global as the Summer Games.

Hosting the Olympics

When the bid to bring the 2012 Olympic Games to London began in 2003, few of those involved dared to believe that it would be successful. To win the vote at the International Olympic Committee's meeting in Singapore in 2005, the London team would have to convince members of the IOC that they would be a better host city than other great cities such as Paris, Madrid, and New York.

Supporters included British Prime Minister Tony Blair, who gave political backing, and soccer star David Beckham, who added glamour. The team worked hard to edge London ahead of the front-runner, Paris. Bid leader and double Olympic gold medalist Lord Sebastian Coe made a passionate presentation about the power of the Olympics to inspire young people around the world to play sports. At last, the IOC members cast their votes. The Games were coming to London.

▲ People celebrate outside Buckingham Palace in London as the Beijing Olympics come to an end in August 2008. At the Beijing closing ceremony, the Olympic flag was passed to London as the next city to host the Games.

THE INTERNATIONAL OLYMPIC COMMITTEE

The IOC leads the **Olympic Movement**, which also includes the National Olympic Committees (NOCs) and the international bodies in charge of each sport. As well as governing the Olympics and promoting sports around the world, the IOC decides where the Games will be held. It has a maximum of 115 members, including active athletes and members of the different parts of the Olympic Movement. The IOC is based in Geneva, Switzerland, and has been led since 2001 by Jacques Rogge, a former Olympic sailor from Belgium.

Awarding the Olympics

After the first modern Olympics had been such a success, many people felt that they should always be held in Athens, Greece. Pierre de Coubertin had other ideas, and the next Games were staged in his home city of Paris. Ever since then, they have been held in different cities. In 2016, the Games will be held in Rio de Janeiro, Brazil. Africa will then be the only continent, apart from Antarctica, that has not yet hosted the Olympics.

Deciding who should host the Games is an important part of the IOC's role. Cities must put forward detailed plans that make clear how they will handle the huge project, and meet the cost of holding the Games. They also need to convince the voters that they will bring something new to the Olympics. With no more than 115 people voting, personal contact and influencing individual members can be very important.

A controversial choice?

The decision about who will host the Games is often controversial. Some people were concerned that Beijing, which hosted the spectacular Games in 2008, should not have been awarded the Olympics. This was because they were critical of the way China governs its people. There have also been suggestions of **corruption** in the past (see page 48).

THE OLYMPIC FLAME

The Olympic flame is a major feature of every Olympic stadium. Some time before the Games, a torch is lit by the sun's rays in Olympia, Greece. The flame is then carried by a relay of runners, each carrying a burning torch, from Olympia to the host city. If it has to cross the sea, the torch is carried by boat or plane. The final runner lights the flame in the stadium during the opening ceremony. It remains alight for the duration of the Olympic Games.

Building the dream

On July 27, 2012, the eyes of the world will be on London, UK, and the opening ceremony of the Olympic Games. As athletes from more than 200 countries parade around the stadium, it will also mark the end of a very long journey for the team responsible for bringing the Games to London for a record third time.

Once the Olympics have been awarded to a city, the real work starts. The London Olympics will be centered in the east of the city, where a new Olympic Park has been created on disused industrial land. This includes the 80,000-seat Olympic Stadium, the Aquatics Centre for swimming and diving, and several other new venues. It also contains an Olympic Village to house around 17,000 athletes and officials.

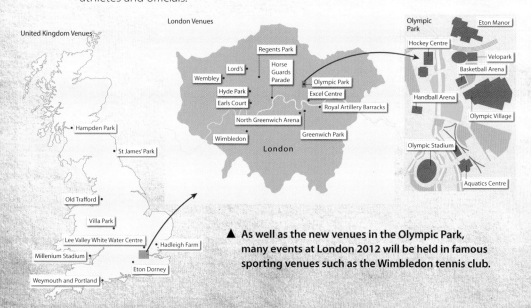

▲ As well as the new venues in the Olympic Park, many events at London 2012 will be held in famous sporting venues such as the Wimbledon tennis club.

The Olympic Stadium is the centerpiece of the Games. It is the venue for the opening and closing ceremonies and athletics events. Other venues need to be found or created for a diverse range of sports, including sailing, mountain biking, and **equestrian** events.

Planning for the future

As well as building the venues for the Games, host cities need to think of the numbers of visitors that the Games will bring. New transportation systems often have to be created to get them to and from the Olympic venues. All this means that the winning host city commits itself to massive costs to stage the Olympics. The 2004 Olympics in Athens were hugely over budget, and many of the expensive new venues were abandoned after the Olympics. The Olympic Games last for just over two weeks. Host cities need to plan for the future after the Games.

GREAT MOMENTS

THE OPENING CEREMONY, BEIJING, CHINA, AUGUST 8, 2008

The Olympic Games begin with an opening ceremony. Athletes parade around the stadium behind an athlete carrying their national flag. The 2008 opening ceremony in Beijing's Bird's Nest Stadium was possibly the most spectacular ever seen. More than 10,000 performers took part in a show that had taken many years of planning. The climax of the event saw gymnast Li Ning appear to run around the rim of the stadium, suspended by wires, to light the Olympic flame with his burning torch.

Olympic Sports

One reason why staging the Olympics is such a huge project is the wide variety of sports that feature in the Games. Many of these sports need purpose-built venues. This variety of sports is what makes the Olympics the world's greatest sporting event, from the explosive speed of sprinting or track cycling, to the power of weightlifting and the skill and precision of shooting or archery.

Track and field

Of the more than 10,000 athletes at the London Olympics, around one-fifth will take part in one of the 47 athletics events. For many people, the Olympics are all about athletics. Some of these events, such as the javelin, can trace their origins back to the ancient Olympic Games at Olympia. The modern version of the ancient *stade* race is the 100-meter sprint. The winners are considered to be the fastest man and woman in the world.

BIOGRAPHY

USAIN BOLT (born 1986)

Usain Bolt was the undisputed star of the Beijing Olympics in 2008. The 6-foot, 5-inch (1.96-meter) Jamaican broke world records and won gold medals in the 100 and 200 meters. Bolt and his teammates also broke the world record in the 4 × 100 meter relay. As much as his amazing running, Bolt's charm and winning smile made him a favorite with audiences around the world. The son of grocers from rural Jamaica, Bolt played cricket and soccer as a child. He has suggested that, after the 2012 Olympics, he may give up athletics to play professional soccer.

Runners, particularly in the sprint events, often carry the hopes of their nation at the Olympics. That responsibility almost guaranteed that American Michael Johnson would become the first man to win the 200 and 400 meters in Atlanta in 1996, and that Australian Cathy Freeman would win the 400 meters a few days after lighting the Olympic flame at the start of the Sydney Games.

TECHNOLOGY

HITTING NEW HEIGHTS

Running, jumping, and throwing events are a pure test of one athlete's speed and strength against another's—or are they? Since the modern Olympic Games started in 1896, athletes have benefited from new technologies such as running spikes and clothes made from very light and flexible materials to help them set new records. Strong, springy, and light **carbon fiber** poles have enabled pole vaulters to leap much higher than their predecessors could with heavy wooden poles. Better understanding of athletes' diets and training methods have also helped Olympic champions to run faster and jump higher.

▲ Technology can also stop athletes from breaking records. During the 1980s, there were concerns that a spectator could be injured as the world record for the javelin throw went over 100 meters. The design of the javelin was changed so it would not fly so far.

Lasting the distance

Distance running has seen some of the greatest performances of the Olympic Games. These events are the ultimate test of strength and endurance. No judges or high-tech equipment can influence the result. It is all about who is the fastest and toughest over 5,000 or 10,000 meters or over the 26 miles and 385 yards (42.2 kilometers) of the marathon.

The marathon is the toughest of athletic events and has given us some of the great Olympic stories, starting with the victory of local hero Spiridon Louis in Athens in 1896. Abebe Bikila became the first African to win the marathon in Rome in 1960, running in bare feet. Bikila won again in 1964, this time with shoes on.

African dominance

At recent Olympics, distance running has been dominated by runners from African countries such as Ethiopia, Kenya, and Morocco. Following in the footsteps of Abebe Bikila, athletes such as Haile Gebrselassie and Tirunesh Dibaba have dominated their events and provided inspiration for the next generation of athletes.

OLYMPIC GREATS

KENENISA BEKELE (born 1982)

Kenenisa Bekele has been called the "unknown superstar." By the time he retires from running, he could well be remembered as the greatest African athlete of all. Bekele has won three Olympic gold medals, including both the 5,000-meter and 10,000-meter titles at the Beijing Olympics. Bekele was born in Ethiopia in 1982, the son of a barley farmer. After winning the 5,000 meters at the Athens Olympics in 2004, tragedy struck Bekele's life. His fiancée, the athlete Alem Techale, collapsed and died while they were out training. Bekele thought about quitting the sport but came back to win double Olympic gold in Beijing. He will be aiming for more medals at the London Olympics in 2012.

MARATHON—NOT LONG ENOUGH?

The standard distance for the marathon is now 26 miles and 385 yards. This was not always the case. At the London Olympics in 1908, the marathon course was 26 miles from Windsor Castle to the Olympic Stadium. Three hundred and eighty-five yards were added so that the athletes would finish in front of Queen Alexandra in the Royal Box. The distance has remained the same ever since.

▲ In 2012, athletes in the marathon will finish in the Mall in front of Buckingham Palace, just as they do in the annual London Marathon.

In the pool

Swimming has been part of every summer Olympics since 1896. In that year, swimming events took place in the sea near Athens. The River Seine was used at the Paris Games in 1900. For the London Olympics, the Aquatics Centre contains two 50-meter pools and a smaller pool for diving.

Small improvements in technique can make a big difference in swimming, as races are often decided by a tiny margin. Swimmers compete in four strokes: freestyle, backstroke, breaststroke, and butterfly, which was added as a separate stroke in 1968. A new event, the 10-kilometer marathon swim, was added at the Beijing Olympics. As well as Michael Phelps, legends of the sport include Mark Spitz and the Australian swimmers Ian Thorpe and Dawn Fraser.

BIOGRAPHY

MICHAEL PHELPS (born 1985)

Michael Phelps' collection of 14 gold medals in Athens and Beijing beats that of every other Olympian, and he could still win more. Phelps was still a teenager when he won six gold medals at the Athens Olympics. In Beijing, Phelps's eight gold medals broke the record of fellow U.S. swimmer Mark Spitz, who won seven golds in Munich in 1972. What is it that makes Phelps such an amazing athlete?

- Body shape: Phelps has a very long body and arms in relation to the length of his legs. This means he has more power and less drag through the water. His size-14 feet also help to drive him forward.
- Recovery time: to win multiple events in a few days, Phelps needs amazing powers of recovery so he is ready for the next race.
- Winning mentality: even great athletes have races where things go wrong or they don't feel so good. When that happens, the will to win takes over.

High divers

Swimming is not the only sport that takes place in the Aquatics Centre. In the diving competition, contenders will make incredibly difficult gymnastic moves look very easy. Synchronized swimmers, in teams or pairs, perform identical gymnastic routines to music. When this sport was introduced to the Olympics in 1984, there was also a solo event!

TECHNOLOGY

BODYSUIT BOOST

Most of the swimmers breaking records at the 2008 Beijing Olympics were wearing high-tech body suits that helped them to move more easily through the water. After the Games, swimming's governing body banned the suits, as they were giving some swimmers an unfair advantage. This may mean that fewer records will be broken in the future, but Olympic sports should be about who is the best athlete, rather than who has the best technology.

▲ Swimmers are often still teenagers when they achieve success in their sport. Nineteen-year-old Briton Rebecca Adlington won two gold medals at the Beijing Games and broke one of the longest-standing world records in the sport for the 400-meter freestyle.

Cycle power

Track cycling on indoor wooden tracks began in the late 1800s and was included in the first modern Olympics. Cyclists still compete on a steeply banked wooden track called a velodrome. Success on the track relies on tactics, as cyclists try to be in the best position to attack, and explosive pace. Great Britain's cyclists won seven of the ten gold medals awarded at the Beijing Olympics, including three golds for Scotland's Chris Hoy in the sprint events.

Other types of cycling at the Olympics include road racing over about 150 miles (240 kilometers) for men and 80 miles (130 kilometers) for women. Mountain biking was introduced to the Olympics in 1996. Mountain bikers have to go around and over obstacles such as tree roots and rocks as they race each other around a cross-country circuit. Bicycle motocross (BMX) was added to the Olympics in 2008, and the thrills and spills of this sport will be on show in the Olympic Park in 2012. The bikes and skills for each of these cycling disciplines are very different.

▲ **BMX became an Olympic sport in Beijing. The cyclists race around an uneven course with tight corners.**

On the water

Cycling is not the only Olympic sport where athletes combine their strength and skill with high-tech equipment. Sports such as sailing and rowing try to ensure that all competitors are using the same equipment so that the event is a true test of who are the best athletes. Sailors race against each other in identical boats with their names and national flags on the sail to identify who is who.

Animal athletes

It is impossible to make all the equipment "identical" in the equestrian events. These are the only Olympic events where humans compete alongside animals. They are also the only events in which men and women compete against each other. The equestrian events at the London Olympics will be held in Greenwich Park.

Dream teams

The Olympics are not just about individuals. Working as a team is an important part of many Olympic sports. Basketball made its Olympic debut at Berlin in 1936. The sand-covered court was outside, and rain turned it into a muddy mess. The United States won gold and did not lose a game until 1972. In 1992, professionals were allowed to compete in the basketball competition for the first time. The U.S. "dream team" of NBA stars such as Michael Jordan duly collected the gold medal. In 2008, the United States won gold again with stars such as Lebron James and Kobe Bryant, after only claiming a bronze medal in Athens. Women's basketball was first seen at the 1976 Olympics, and the U.S. women's team has dominated recent tournaments.

Men's and women's soccer both feature in the Olympics. The Olympic soccer tournament was first staged in London in 1908, making it older than the World Cup. Until 1992, only amateurs were allowed to play, so most of soccer's greatest stars never appeared at the Olympics. From 1996, the rules have been changed so that professionals are allowed as long as no more than three in any team are older than 23. Argentina's gold-medal winning team in 2008 featured many young stars, including Lionel Messi.

Amateur or professional?

For most of their history, the modern Olympics have insisted that they were only for amateur sportspeople. Ski instructors were even banned from taking part in the Winter Olympics because they were classed as professionals. However, during the 1980s it became more difficult to draw a line between amateur and professional, as athletes were supported by government funding or commercial sponsors. In 1987 the IOC decided to bring back tennis, which had been an Olympic sport until 1924. Tennis's multimillionaire professionals were allowed to compete, and most sports now allow professionals.

▲ Steve Redgrave won gold medals at five Olympics between 1984 and 2000. Winning even one gold medal in rowing is a result of individual strength, endurance, and great teamwork.

CASSIUS CLAY WINS BOXING GOLD, ROME, ITALY, SEPTEMBER 1960

Boxing is one sport where only amateurs can take part in the Olympics. African American Cassius Clay won Olympic gold as an amateur in 1960. Changing his name to Muhammad Ali, he went on to become one of the greatest-ever sportsmen. Clay was so proud of his gold medal that he wore it all the time. He even slept with it around his neck. However, when he was refused service in a whites-only restaurant, Clay threw his medal into a river in disgust. He overcame Parkinson's disease to light the Olympic flame in Atlanta in 1996, where the IOC also presented him with a replacement medal.

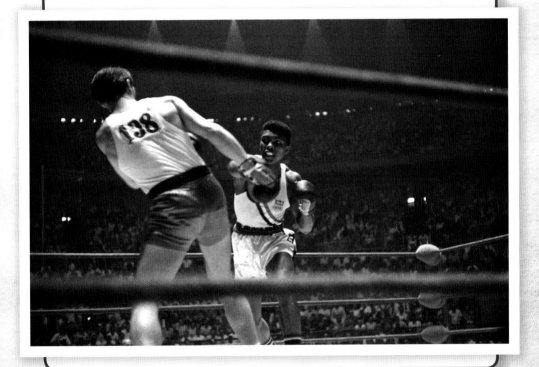

Although allowing professionals to compete has meant that the best athletes in the world can compete at the Olympics, many people still think that the Olympics should be for sports where an Olympic medal is the ultimate achievement. People argue that the Olympics are just another tournament for stars of soccer, basketball, and tennis. For a young track-and-field athlete or rower, that Olympic gold medal is the ultimate prize.

"I never knew that was an Olympic sport"

Sports such as athletics, swimming, and cycling are known by everyone. They attract competitors from around the world. At the London Olympics, there will be a total of 26 different sports with more than 300 different events. Not all of them are quite so well known.

Fencing began as long ago as the 17th century, when blunt swords and facemasks made of wire mesh were used for sword practice. At the Olympics, fencers are attached to an electronic scoring system so that any touch from their opponent's weapon is registered automatically. In the 1924 Olympics, the Italian and Hungarian fencing teams settled an argument with a real-life duel. Fortunately, the fencing competition has calmed down a bit since then.

Trampolining will be the newest sport at the London Olympics. It first appeared in Sydney in 2000. A total of just 32 competitors (16 men and 16 women) compete for the two gold medals in trampolining. In addition to the well-known and widely popular artistic gymnastics, athletes will also compete in rhythmic gymnastics, which is a combination of dance and gymnastics.

BEHIND THE SCENES

WHO'S IN AND WHO'S OUT?

Sports can be added or removed from the Olympics. Inclusion in the Olympics can make a big difference to a sport. Governments will often give funding to athletes in minority sports if they are part of the Olympics. There will be no new sports in 2012. In 2009, the IOC voted to include golf in the 2016 Rio de Janeiro Games. Rugby sevens (pictured) is a short version of rugby that has seven members on each team instead of 15. Members of the IOC's executive committee selected those sports ahead of squash, karate, baseball, and softball. The last two were dropped from the Olympics after 2008. Baseball's case was damaged by the fact that top stars do not play in the Olympics as they are playing for their professional teams in summer.

▲ In tug-of-war, two opposing teams try to pull the rope six feet in their own direction. Controversy erupted in 1908 when the U.S. team accused a team of policemen from Liverpool of wearing illegal boots. The last Olympic tug-of-war was in 1920.

Discontinued sports

Although baseball and softball were the first sports to be removed from the Games program since polo in 1936, early Olympic Games included many unusual events.

- Cricket is a popular sport in many countries but only featured once at the Olympic Games. In 1900, Great Britain was beaten by a French team containing several players from the British Embassy in Paris. While a French magazine called the game "monotonous and without color," the British saw things differently. One British report said, "the French temperament is too excitable … and no Frenchman can be persuaded to play the game more than once."

- The 1900 Olympics in Paris also included a swimming obstacle race and the long jump on horseback.

- Other discontinued sports include croquet, *jeu de paume* ("real tennis"), polo, and motor boating.

Winter sports

The Winter Olympics were introduced in 1924. The first Winter Games in Chamonix, France, included Nordic or cross-country skiing, bobsled, ice hockey, speed skating, and ice skating. Since then, many sports have been added, most notably alpine skiing events such as downhill and slalom in 1936. Today, the Winter Olympics also include exciting sports such as snowboarding. Ski cross was a new feature at Vancouver 2010.

High-speed sports

Winter Olympic sliding sports are some of the fastest sports in the Olympics. Athletes in luge, skeleton, and bobsled travel at around 90 miles (145 kilometers) per hour down a concrete chute covered in ice. Bobsledders are protected by a fiberglass capsule, but luge and skeleton athletes are only protected by helmets and have no brakes.

Speed skaters are no slouches either. They compete over distances between 500 and 10,000 meters at speeds up to 60 miles (97 kilometers) per hour. Speed skaters compete against a single opponent in each race. Short track skating is similar to speed skating, but all the skaters race together around tighter corners. With so many skaters at high speed, crashes are common.

The Winter Olympics are not just about thrills and spills. Cross-country skiing at distances up to 31 miles (50 kilometers) is a huge test of stamina as arms and legs are used to push the skier through the snow. Figure skating is all about combining the most difficult tricks on ice into a graceful routine.

Canada's game?

Ice hockey is one of the toughest sports on ice. Players wear plenty to protect them from the rubber puck, which they are trying to hit into the goal at high speed. However, the protection is also to guard them against other players. Holding, tripping, or obstructing an opponent are not legal, but body-checking with the shoulder or hip is allowed. Ice hockey is the number one sport in Canada, so the pressure was on for the Canadian team to succeed at the Vancouver Winter Olympics in 2010. The country went wild when Canada beat the United States 3–2 in overtime to win gold.

GREAT MOMENTS

FIVE GREAT WINTER OLYMPICS PERFORMANCES

- Bjorn Daehlie (Norway, 1992–1998): More Winter Olympic golds than anyone else (eight) and twelve medals in total in some of the toughest events—cross-country skiing at distances up to 32 miles (50 kilometers).

- Eric Heiden (USA, 1976–1980): Won all five gold medals in speed skating in 1980. After finishing skating, Heiden became a professional cyclist and competed in the Tour de France.

- Janica Kostelic (Croatia, 1998–2006): More medals than any other woman in Alpine skiing. Kostelic also appears on a Croatian postage stamp.

- Jayne Torvill and Christopher Dean (UK, 1984 and 1994): Only one gold medal, but the ice dancers achieved perfection with a clean sweep of maximum 6.0 marks for artistic impression in Sarajevo, 1984.

- Shaun White (USA, 2006–2010): Two Winter Olympics and two gold medals in the snowboard half-pipe. Will the "Flying Tomato" be back for more in Sochi, Russia, in 2014? White is also a champion skateboarder.

▲ **Shaun White won the snowboard half-pipe in Vancouver 2010.**

Paralympic sports

Many people associate the Paralympic Games with wheelchair athletics. Those sports are certainly an important part of the Games, but there is much more to the Paralympics. Twenty sports will feature at the London Paralympics, from Paralympic versions of Olympic sports such as sailing to sports that only feature at the Paralympics, such as boccia.

Boccia is played by athletes with severe **cerebral palsy** and other nerve disorders. Athletes must throw balls to try and finish closest to a target ball or jack. Extreme muscle control and precision are the keys to success. Another sport that only features at the Paralympics is goalball. Unlike most Olympic and Paralympic sports, spectators at a goalball game are totally silent. This is essential so that the **visually impaired** players can hear the bells inside the ball that tell them where it is. The aim is to throw the ball into the opposing team's goal while players try to block the throw with their bodies.

▲ Wheelchair tennis player Esther Vergeer is one of the most amazing athletes in any sport. Up to 2008, she had won five Paralympic golds (three in singles, two in doubles) and by the end of 2010 had gone for seven years without losing a match.

Paralympic classification

Although some Paralympic sports, like the two mentioned on page 42, are specific to athletes with certain disabilities, many sports such as athletics and swimming feature athletes with a wide range of disabilities, from visually impaired athletes to **amputees** or those with spinal injuries. The Paralympic Movement has had to come up with a way of grouping athletes in different events according to their disabilities. This is done using a system of classification that groups athletes according to five major groups: amputees, cerebral palsy, spinal injuries, visually impaired athletes, and those not covered by the other groups. This means that the Paralympics actually contain more medal events than the Summer Olympics.

The level of competition at the Paralympics is just as high as at the Olympics. More than 140 countries sent athletes to the Beijing Paralympics in 2008. Paralympians are highly trained athletes, who happen to have a disability. The London Paralympics should be the biggest ever, with more than 4,000 athletes attending.

BIOGRAPHY

OSCAR PISTORIUS (born 1986)

Pistorius gets his nickname "the blade runner" from his artificial legs made from carbon fiber and wood. Both of his legs were amputated below the knee before he was a year old, but that has not stopped him from becoming an amazing athlete. Pistorius did not let his disability stop him from playing rugby and water polo at school. He won gold in the 200-meter sprint at the 2004 Athens Paralympics just a few months after taking up athletics. At Beijing in 2008, he won three gold medals, at 100, 200, and 400 meters. Pistorius is hoping to compete in both the Olympics and Paralympics in 2012. He says that his artificial legs are light but very uncomfortable.

Controversy at the Olympics

The Olympics is one of very few events or movements where almost every country in the world is represented. In any race or event there could be athletes from countries that are hostile or even at war with each other. The Games are also the most watched television event around the world. Any crisis or disagreement at the Games becomes a global issue. The sheer number of nations and different interests involved means that the Olympics have experienced their share of conflict and controversy.

Many of the following issues extend over a long period, covering several Olympics, and some are likely to continue as long as athletes meet to compete for Olympic gold medals.

Cheating at the Olympics

There are no short cuts to becoming an Olympic champion. Athletes have to prepare in minute detail and train hard for many years in order to come out on top against those who have as much or more talent. However, the problem of athletes trying to cheat their way to a gold medal has been present throughout the Games' history.

Some of the earlier attempts at cheating are almost comic now. Fred Lorz, who finished first in the marathon in 1904, was disqualified when it was discovered he had taken a lift in a truck—he would have finished sooner but the truck broke down. Soviet athlete Boris Onischenko was sent home in disgrace in 1976 when he was found to be using a fencing épée (type of sword) in the modern pentathlon that contained a switch to register false hits on the electronic scoring system.

Even the Paralympics are not immune. In 2000, the Spanish basketball team for players with learning difficulties had their gold medals taken away when it was found that most of them did not suffer from the disabilities they claimed.

Performance-enhancing drugs

In modern times, the main way of cheating has been by using drugs to improve performance. The IOC began testing athletes for use of drugs in 1972, but for many people drugs really became an issue in 1988. At the Seoul Olympics of that year, Canada's Ben Johnson broke the world record to finish ahead of Carl Lewis in the 100 meters. It was an astonishing run. Viewers around the world were even more astonished when it was announced that Johnson had tested positive for drugs after the race.

▲ Ben Johnson's drug-assisted run in Seoul, South Korea, brought home to many people the prevalence of drug use in some sports.

BEHIND THE SCENES

CATCHING THE DRUG-USING CHEATERS

Catching drug-using cheaters has become a priority for the Olympic Movement. Athletes are regularly tested outside competition and during major competitions. They must provide a urine sample, which is split into two separate A and B samples. If an A sample is found to contain drugs, the B sample is then tested to confirm the result. More than 5,000 samples will be tested at the London Olympics and 1,200 at the Paralympics. New drugs and masking agents, which can stop other drugs from being detected, are developed all the time. The challenge for the authorities is to stay ahead of these developments.

Ben Johnson was not the first or last athlete to be caught using drugs. U.S. sprinter Marion Jones was stripped of her five Olympic medals and banned for using drugs, and suspicion has fallen on many other athletes. Other sports that have been affected include road cycling and weightlifting. East German teams are believed to have used drugs extensively in the 1980s.

Effects of drug use

No one knows exactly what proportion of drug-using cheaters get caught. The effects of drug use are serious for the individual and for their sports. There are Olympic champions who used drugs but were never caught. Not only do they have medals that they won unfairly; other athletes have also been denied the medals that are rightfully theirs. The sports themselves are also damaged if spectators doubt the truth of a record-breaking performance. Performance-enhancing drugs can also affect an athlete's own health. There are several examples of athletes who have died of health problems related to drug use.

Peace and conflict

For many years, particularly during the Cold War, the Olympics were affected by political concerns between nations. Since the last big boycott in 1984, this has been less of a problem. However, with so many nations competing, the Olympics are inevitably affected by what's happening in the world. One of the most positive effects the Olympics have had was in South Korea. The awarding of the Games to Seoul in 1988 was a major factor in persuading the Korean government to hold democratic elections.

The staging of the Olympics in Beijing, China, in 2008 was seen by many as recognizing the changing status of China in the world. The spectacular opening ceremony and the fact that Chinese athletes topped the medals table also showed the wealth and power of China.

In the 21st century, terrorism and security are major concerns for the Olympics. The Games were a target for terrorists in 1972 and, to a lesser extent, at Atlanta in 1996. Fear of terrorist attacks has increased the cost of staging such a huge event. The day after London was awarded the Olympic Games in 2005, terrorists attacked London's public transportation system, killing many people. Terrorists will target events where they can get maximum publicity. There is no more high-profile event than the Olympics, and this makes the Games a possible target.

▲ A bus was one of the vehicles destroyed in London on July 7, 2005. More than 50 people were killed and 700 were injured during morning rush-hour terrorist attacks on the day after London was awarded the Olympic Games.

BEHIND THE SCENES

OLYMPIC SECURITY

Security is a major headache and cost for Olympic organizers. Rising security costs after terrorist attacks on the United States in 2001 were a major reason why the Athens Olympics in 2004 cost more than planned. London is expecting hundreds of thousands of additional visitors in 2012, as well as the athletes and officials taking part in the Games. The organizing committee needs to include several hundred million dollars in their budgets to cover security.

Money and media

As well as being a huge event for athletes and sports fans around the world, the Olympics are also big business. Host cities hope to benefit from increased interest and visitors to their city, but they also have to cover the huge cost of staging the Games. The Olympic Movement benefits from charging television companies to show the Olympics. This is called selling them the rights. Businesses from banks to soft drink companies will pay a lot of money to advertise or be linked in other ways with the Olympics. This guarantees them an audience around the world and association with the positive values of the Olympics.

Not everyone is happy about the number and types of businesses involved in the Olympics. Some people argue that businesses such as soft drink or fast food companies do not promote the healthy lifestyle that should be associated with the Olympics. Supporters of business involvement point out that staging the Olympics is very costly, and no one could afford to host the event without working with businesses.

Corruption

Big money in the Olympics has also led to allegations that some host cities have resorted to illegal means to win the race to host the Olympics. In 1998, it emerged that IOC delegates had received payments and gifts from Salt Lake City, Utah, in exchange for their votes in favor of the city's bid to host the Winter Olympics. One IOC member from Togo, which is not known for its winter sports, was invited to visit Salt Lake City on two occasions. In 1999, four IOC members resigned and six were expelled over the issue. It was also clear that Salt Lake City was not the only bidding city that was prepared to buy votes. Since then, the IOC has brought in new rules, and members are not allowed to visit host cities.

The Olympics will always have to deal with controversies like these. This is partly because of the size of the Games, but also because Pierre de Coubertin and other founders of the Olympic Movement wanted the Olympics to be more than just another sporting event. The Olympic Movement has to constantly try to preserve the values that make the Olympics so special.

▲ Double gold-medalist Michael Johnson provided great publicity for sportswear company Nike, who provided his gold running shoes at Atlanta in 1996.

BEHIND THE SCENES

TELEVISION RIGHTS

Unless we are lucky enough to live near an Olympic host city and get tickets to the Games, most of us will follow the Olympics on television and on the Internet. The 1948 London Olympics were broadcast to viewers in the United Kingdom, although at that time very few people had televisions. The 2012 Olympics will be broadcast to people in more than 200 countries. Television rights for Beijing 2008 were sold for over $1.6 billion. Just over half of this money was paid by a U.S. television company. Many people complain that TV companies have too much power over the Games. This includes influencing the timing of events for when more people will be watching in the United States or Europe. The companies' supporters argue that the money paid for TV rights makes the Games possible and supports sports around the world.

The Meaning of the Olympics

The strong values that were behind the founding of the Olympic Games also partly explain its enduring global success. The Olympic movement aims to use sports to promote peace and links between cultures, and to build enjoyment in taking part in sports.

Olympic symbols

The Olympic Movement and the Olympic Games are associated with many powerful symbols that express the values of the Games. The pursuit of excellence is symbolized by the Olympic motto. This Latin motto is "Citius, Altius, Fortius," which means "Faster, Higher, Stronger."

BIOGRAPHY

SEBASTIAN COE (born 1956)

If Sebastian Coe had not done anything since the Los Angeles Olympics in 1984, he would still be an Olympic great. Coe won gold in the 1,500 meters and silver in the 800 meters in 1980 and 1984 for the UK. After retiring from athletics, Coe went into politics. As Lord Coe, he went on to lead the organizing committee for the London Olympics. His understanding and passion for the Olympic Movement made him a key figure in bringing the Games to London in 2012.

GREAT MOMENTS

ERIC MOUSSAMBANI, SYDNEY, AUSTRALIA, 2000

For all the athletes who win multiple gold medals, there are others who go down in history simply for representing the values of the Olympics. Eric Moussambani arrived at the Sydney Olympics having only taken up swimming a few months earlier. Moussambani's training facility back home in Equatorial Guinea had been a 20-meter hotel pool that he could use when it was not being used by hotel guests. After two

other swimmers in his heat were disqualified, Moussambani had to swim the 100-meter freestyle alone. He had never swum the distance before. As he neared the end, it looked like he might not make it. The roar of the crowd kept him going. His time was 50 seconds slower than the next slowest athlete.

The Olympic flag is recognized around the world. It was designed by Pierre de Coubertin and symbolizes all the nations that meet at the Olympic Games. The five interlocking rings represent the five continents. The colors of the rings and the white background appear in the flags of every nation in the world. The flag was designed after the Stockholm Olympics in 1912, which were the first Games at which all five continents were represented.

Apart from the flag, the symbol that most people associate with the Olympic Games is the Olympic flame. After its journey from Olympia, the flame is lit during the opening ceremony. It symbolizes the history of the Olympics and the links to the ancient Games at Olympia.

Another link to the Games' ancient origins is the Olympic **oath**, in which one athlete promises to respect the rules on behalf of all the other athletes. The athlete takes the oath during the opening ceremony. An oath was also taken at the ancient Olympics.

After the Olympics

As well as staging a great sporting festival, cities that bid for the Olympics also want the Games to have a lasting impact on their city and its people. There are many ways in which this legacy can be achieved.

▲ The London Olympic Stadium will welcome 80,000 people on July 27, 2012, for the opening ceremony of the Olympic Games.

Most Olympic bids involve building several new sporting venues. Buildings such as the Olympic Village are built to house the athletes and officials during the Games. Some venues will be temporary, but others will remain for many years after the Games. London has built an Olympic Park that includes not just sporting venues, but also habitats for animals and plants. This should remain as a park for Londoners long after the Olympics have finished. New transportation links have also been built, and the Olympic Village will be converted to housing after the Games.

The athletes will hope that the legacy of the Games is sporting success for them. For some, their measure of success may be nothing less than a gold medal. Others will be happy just to compete at the Games, or to make the final in their sport. Many will also make new friendships with other athletes from around the world.

The story continues

The most important legacy of the Games will be to inspire people around the world to take up sports and adopt the values of the Olympic Movement. This will keep the Olympics growing into the future. After the London Olympics in 2012, the next Winter Olympics will take place in Sochi, Russia, in 2014. At the end of the London Olympics, the Olympic flag will be passed to the next home of the Summer Olympics, Rio de Janeiro, Brazil, for the first South American Olympics.

The Olympic Creed

"The most important thing in life is not the triumph, but the fight; the essential thing is not to have won, but to have fought well."

The creed was written by Pierre de Coubertin, based on the words of the Bishop of Pennsylvania in 1908.

GREAT MOMENTS

INSPIRING FUTURE OLYMPIANS

Many athletes speak of the time they were inspired to aim for Olympic gold. Sebastian Coe has spoken of the inspiration of watching the Mexico City Olympics in 1968, when he was 12 years old. As the Olympic Games unfold in London in 2012, there will be many great sporting moments. The seeds will also be planted for future Olympic champions, as young people around the world are inspired by what they see.

Olympic Records

Athletes

Most Olympic medals:
- Summer Olympics: Gymnast Larisa Latynina (Soviet Union) won 18 medals, including 9 gold medals, between 1956 and 1964.
- Winter Olympics: Bjorn Daehlie (Norway) won 12 medals in cross-country skiing between 1992 and 1998.

Most Olympic gold medals:
- Summer Olympics: Michael Phelps (USA) won 14 gold medals in swimming, at Athens (2004) and Beijing (2008).
- Winter Olympics: Bjorn Daehlie (Norway) won 8 gold medals as part of his total medal record (see above).
- Eddie Eagan (USA) is the only athlete to have won gold medals at the Summer (1920, for boxing) and Winter Olympics (1932, for bobsledding).

Oldest medalists:
- Oscar Swahn (Sweden) won a silver medal for shooting in 1920 at the age of 72 years and 279 days.
- The oldest female medalist was Sybil "Queenie" Newell (UK), who won a gold medal in archery in 1908 at the age of 53 years and 277 days.

Youngest medalists:
- Dimitrious Loundrous (Greece) was 10 years and 218 days old when he finished third in a gymnastics event in 1896. There were no bronze medals awarded at that time and, in this event, third was also last.
- Inge Sorensen (Denmark) won the 200-meter breaststroke at Berlin in 1936 to become the Olympics' youngest individual medalist. She was 12 years and 24 days old.
- Eleanor Simmonds (pictured) became Great Britain's youngest Paralympic medalist when she won two gold medals in Beijing in 2008 at the age of 13.

Countries

Most medals at the Summer Olympic Games

Country	Gold	Silver	Bronze
United States	943	736	642
Soviet Union (competed between 1924 and 1988)	395	319	296
United Kingdom	216	272	257
France	211	225	258
Italy	203	168	178
Germany (excludes separate East and West Germany teams between 1968 and 1988)	202	229	253
Hungary	162	148	163
East Germany (competed between 1968 and 1988)	153	129	127
Sweden	143	165	181
Australia	131	140	168

Source: www.sports-reference.com/olympics

Finland has won more Olympic medals relative to its population than any other country, with more than 500 medals for every 1 million people. The United Kingdom is 20th on the list, and Australia is 12th. The United States is ranked 28th, just ahead of Canada in 29th place.

Countries that topped the medal table

Summer Olympics

Olympic Games	Leading country	Gold	Silver	Bronze
2008 Beijing, China	China	51	21	28
2004 Athens, Greece	United States	36	39	27
2000 Sydney, Australia	United States	37	24	33
1996 Atlanta, USA	United States	44	32	25

Source: www.sports-reference.com/olympics

Winter Olympics

Olympic Games	Leading country	Gold	Silver	Bronze
2010 Vancouver, Canada	Canada	14	7	5
2006 Turin, Italy	Germany	11	12	6
2002 Salt Lake City, USA	Norway	13	5	7
1998 Nagano, Japan	Germany	12	9	8

Source: www.sports-reference.com/olympics

Timeline of the Olympics

776 BCE   First recorded staging of the ancient Olympic Games in Olympia, Greece

393 CE   Likely date for the end of the ancient Olympics, when Roman emperor Theodosius I banned all non-Christian cults

1766   Olympia rediscovered by Englishman Richard Chandler

1875   Full-scale excavation of the site at Olympia by the German government

1894   International Athletic Conference meets in Paris and agrees to revive the Olympic Games

1896   First modern Olympic Games staged in Athens, Greece, with competitors from 14 nations. The Games are held every four years.

1900   Second Olympic Games held in Paris to coincide with the World's Fair. Women athletes compete for the first time.

1904   First Games outside Europe held in St. Louis, Missouri. Many events only include American athletes.

1908   Olympic Games staged in London for the first time. The first Olympic Stadium is built specifically for the Games.

1920   Olympic flag and Olympic oath make their first appearance at the Antwerp Olympics

1924   First Winter Olympics held in Chamonix, France

1936   Summer and Winter Olympic Games held in Berlin and Garmisch-Partenkirchen, Germany, which was then ruled by Hitler's Nazi government. African American Jesse Owens wins four gold medals.

1948   "Austerity Olympics" held in London after gap of 12 years due to World War II. Games for disabled athletes held in Stoke Mandeville, in the UK, are the forerunner of the Paralympics.

1956   Olympic Games held in the Southern Hemisphere for the first time in Melbourne, Australia. Equestrian events held in Sweden due to Australia's laws on importing animals.

1960   Paralympic Games held for the first time following the Rome Olympics

1964   Tokyo, Japan, stages the first Olympic Games in Asia

1972   Eleven Israeli athletes are killed in a terrorist attack at the Munich Olympics

1980   Sixty-five countries, including the United States, boycott the Olympic Games in Moscow in protest of the Soviet Union's invasion of Afghanistan. This is the largest Olympic boycott.

1992   Barcelona Olympics. Professionals are allowed to compete in many sports for the first time.

1994   Olympic schedule is changed so Winter Olympics are no longer held in the same year as the Summer Olympics. The Winter Olympics are held in Lillehammmer, Norway.

2000   Millennium Games in Sydney, Australia. Steve Redgrave becomes Great Britain's greatest Olympian by winning gold medals for rowing in five different Olympics.

2008   Most expensive Olympic Games ever are held in Beijing, China. Michael Phelps wins eight gold medals.

2012   Summer Olympic Games held in London for the third time

Olympic Host Cities

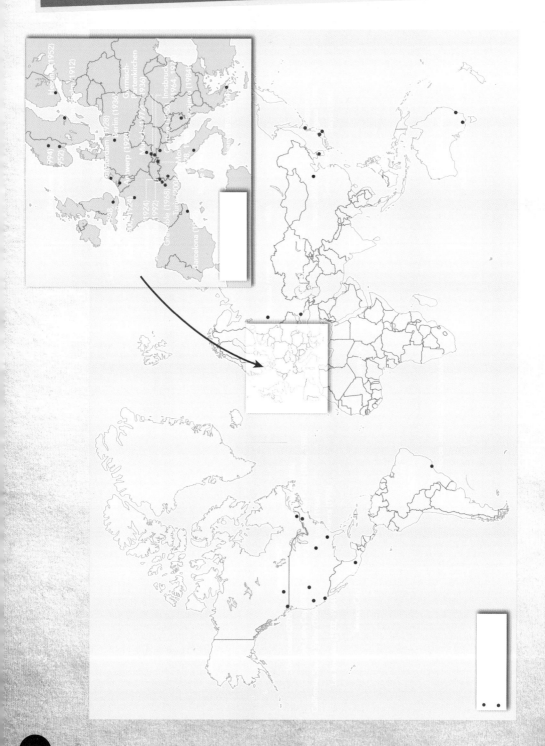

Olympic Sports

Sports that will feature at the London 2012 Summer Olympics
archery
athletics
badminton
basketball
beach volleyball
boxing
canoeing
cycling
equestrian
fencing
gymnastics
handball
hockey
judo
modern pentathlon
rowing
sailing
soccer
swimming (including diving, synchronized swimming, water polo)
table tennis
taekwondo
tennis
triathlon
volleyball
weightlifting
wrestling

Sports featured at the Vancouver 2010 Winter Olympics
Alpine skiing
biathlon
bobsled
cross-country skiing
curling
figure skating
freestyle skiing
ice hockey
luge
Nordic combined
short-track speed skating
skeleton
ski jumping
snowboarding
speed skating

Find Out More

Books

Burs, Kylie. *Alpine and Freestyle Skiing* (Winter Olympic Sports). New York: Crabtree, 2010. (Part of a series with books on many Winter Olympic sports.)

Christopher, Matt. *The Olympics: Legendary Sports Events*. New York: Little, Brown and Co., 2008.

DK Publishing, ed. *The Sports Book*. New York: Dorling Kindersley, 2007.

Morris, Neil. *Should Substance-Using Athletes Be Banned for Life?* (What Do You Think?). Chicago: Heinemann Library, 2009.

Olympic Museum, ed. *Treasures of the Olympic Games*. London: Carlton Books, 2008.

Schweitzer, Karen. *Shaun White* (Role Model Athletes). Broomall, PA: Mason Crest, 2009.

Films

You can find video footage of many great Olympic performances online. The website of the International Olympic Committee (www.olympic.org) is a good place to start.

There have been many films telling stories about the Olympic Games. Some are inspiring, but others tell the story of some of the Olympics' darkest moments.

Chariots of Fire (1981): Two British athletes' quest to win gold at the 1924 Paris Olympics. This film does a great job of capturing the character of the early Olympics.

Cool Runnings (1993): The story of the unlikely Jamaican bobsled team in training for the Calgary Olympics.

One Day in September (1999): This documentary film tells the story of the attack on the Munich Olympics in 1972 by Palestinian terrorists. This film deals with one of the darkest moments in Olympic history, and viewers should be aware that it deals with some shocking issues.

Web resources

www.olympic.org is the website of the International Olympic Committee and a great source of information about athletes, sports, and past Olympic Games.

http://www.olympic.org/museum is a great resource for finding out about the history of the Olympics.

www.teamUSA.org is the website of the U.S. Olympic Committee. National Olympic bodies around the world have their own websites, such as **www.olympic.ca**, the website of the Canadian Olympic Committee.

The main website of the Paralympic Movement is **www.paralympic.org**, and individual countries have their own Paralympic websites such as **www.usparalympics.org**.

www.london2012.com is the website of the London Olympics and includes details of venues and preparations for the London Games, as well as information about Olympic sports.

The British Museum is home to many painted vases and other objects that tell us about sports in ancient Greece. Find out more at **http://www.britishmuseum.org/ explore/families_and_children/online_tours/sport_in_ancient_greece/sport_in_ ancient_greece.aspx**.

Places to visit

The main Olympic Museum is in Lausanne, Switzerland (see website information above). Many past Olympic cities have museums devoted to the Olympics, such as the Centennial Olympic Games Museum in Atlanta, Georgia. You can also see Olympic sporting venues if you live close to a city that has hosted the Olympics.

The ancient Olympic site at Olympia, Greece, is also a great place to visit if you have the chance.

London's Olympic Park is in the east of the city.

Sources and bibliography

The following books and websites have been used in the writing of this book:

Swaddling, Judith. *The Ancient Olympic Games, 3rd edition.* London: British Museum Press, 2004.

Miller, David. *Athens to Athens: The Official History of the Olympic Games and the IOC.* Mainstream Publishing, 2003.

Wallechinsky, David, and Jaime Loucky. *The Complete Book of the Olympics.* Aurum Press, 2008.

Encyclopaedia Britannica, revised edition. London: Encyclopaedia Britannica (UK) Limited, 2009.

www.london-2012.com

www.olympic.org

www.paralympic.org

www.sports-reference.com/olympics

News websites, including:
    www.bbc.co.uk/news
    www.guardian.co.uk
    www.thetimes.co.uk/tto/news

Glossary

Aboriginal having ancestors who have lived in a country since the earliest times. Australia's Aboriginal people lived there long before settlers arrived from Europe.

amateur someone who is not paid for doing something such as playing a sport

amputee person who has lost an arm or a leg

apartheid system of government that existed in South Africa during the 20th century, where different groups of people were segregated and had different rights according to their race

boycott refuse to attend something or deal with another group, such as for political reasons

carbon fiber light but very strong material used in a lot of high-tech sporting equipment

cerebral palsy disability where a person finds it difficult to control his or her limbs

city-state small country made up of a city and the land around it, with its own government. Ancient Greece was made up of several city-states.

corruption breaking rules or laws, such as by taking bribes

disqualified stopped from being part of a race or competition because of breaking the rules

equestrian on horseback or relating to horses

excavation act of digging beneath the ground to uncover remains from the past

human rights rights that every person has, regardless of who they are or where they live

International Olympic Committee (IOC) organization that runs the Olympic Games and decides where they will be held

medal table table showing which countries have won the most medals at the Olympic Games. Countries compete to be top of the medal table.

oath promise, often made in public

Olympic Movement all the people involved in the Olympic Games, including the International Olympic Committee and Olympic officials from each country and each Olympic sport

Paralympic Games games for athletes with a disability, held after the Olympic Games in the same place

pentathlon Olympic event where athletes have to compete in five sports. The modern pentathlon comprises running, horse-riding, shooting, fencing, and swimming.

professional person who earns money for doing something, such as playing a sport

racist judging people based on where they come from and the color of their skin

revive bring back to life

sacred of religious significance

Soviet Union country made up of what is now Russia, Ukraine, and several other countries. The Soviet Union opposed the United States and its allies in the Cold War. The country broke up in 1991.

Sparta city-state in ancient Greece that was known for its tough warriors

spinal injury injury to a person's spinal cord that means that the lower part of the body becomes paralyzed

sponsor pay money to support something. Companies may sponsor an athlete or event as a form of advertising

stade length of a race at the ancient Olympics, equivalent to just over 210 yards (192 meters)

symbolize representing something else, such as a value or an idea

terrorist person who uses violence against the public for political or religious reasons

truce temporary agreement to stop war or conflict

visually impaired have a disability affecting the eyes, such as total loss of sight

Index